THE ROOM IN-BETWEEN

THE ROOM IN-BETWEEN

By
Ana María Delgado

Translated by
Sylvia Ehrlich Lipp

Latin American Literary Review Press
Series: Discoveries
Pittsburgh, Pennsylvania
1995

The Latin American Literary Review Press publishes Spanish language creative writing under the series title *Discoveries*, and critical works under the series title *Explorations*.

Library of Congress Cataloging-in-Publication Data

Delgado, Ana María, 1925
    [Habitacíon de por medio. English]
    The room in-between / by Ana María Delgado;
    translated by Sylvia Ehrlich Lipp.
       p. cm. -- (Series Discoveries)
    ISBN 0-935480-76-5
    I. Lipp, Sylvia Ehrlich. II. Title. III. Series: Discoveries.
    PQ7440. D38H3313   1995
    863--dc20

                                 95-9455
                                 CIP

Cover art by Lisette Miller.

The Room In-Between may be ordered directly from the publisher:

Latin American Literary Review Press
121 Edgewood Avenue • Pittsburgh, PA 15218
Tel: (412)371-9023 • Fax: (412)371-9025

Acknowledgments

This project is supported in part by grants from the National Endowment for the Arts in Washington, D.C., a federal agency, and the Commonwealth of Pennsylvania Council on the Arts.

TO SOLI

Dearest of dears
Husband and friend
These many years

THE ROOM IN-BETWEEN

I tip-toe into your room, not because I'm afraid of making noise but because my old fear of you clutches at me. I'm uncertain about how you will receive me and I must confess it worries me. I approach you slowly, advancing toward the bed where you are lying under a mosquito netting which is draped atop a big box-like contraption, a white gauze, covering and protecting you. Standing there I call to you and though you do not answer, I say:

"I arrived a half hour ago."

You still do not move, but I continue:

"I stayed outside for a while sitting on the steps, getting a breath of fresh air, trying to get rid of a headache which has been bothering me all day."

I'm lying; that was not the reason. What I wanted was to clear my head, to prepare myself for the encounter. I move closer to your bed and see the outline of your body through the mosquito netting. I palpate the ravages of your illness with my eyes, not my hands, which refuse to touch you. I find you enervated, desiccated and consumed by old age which appears to have overwhelmed you by surprise, bringing you down precipitously.

I am not certain that you are asleep but wish to believe you are. I hope you are not pretending. I have no desire to judge you, but it could be another one of your tricks, a time-getting device to give you the opportunity to study me from over there, from the hiding place behind your paper-thin lids. If I am not mistaken, you are at this very moment taking everything in and are quite aware of my presence at your side. You must have heard the chair squeak when I sat down. Besides, when I was speaking to you, my voice must have reached you head-on. Surely you smelled my perfume and must be thinking that I'm still overly concerned with clothing and appearance. If you are not pretending and you are conscious of my presence (I am well acquainted with your inquisitive nature), I assume you are assessing the tone of my voice to ferret out hidden meanings. In all probability you do hear me, but you can't believe your ears. My voice is no longer vibrant or resilient. It is solemn and husky now and sounds like a prematurely-aging church bell. If at last you do me the kindness of looking at me, you will observe the wreck I have become. But you don't open your eyes...and I persist:

"Mama...Mamita," I call softly to you.

There is no response, not even a ripple of movement to indicate that you are listening.

"I plan to stay for a couple of days," I tell you even though you may not be listening.

I tell you that when I received Sara's letter, I was dressing to go out. Then I left and was gone all afternoon. It was only when I returned and saw the letter on top of my dresser that I thought about you again and decided to come see you."

"Do you want to know something? I ask raising my

voice in the hope that you will hear me.

"I had already planned to come visit you before I received the news that you were sick, but with one thing and another, I kept postponing. Now that I know..."

I choke up and in spite of myself, my voice breaks and I don't want you to notice.

"Sorry," I continue, "I had a cold and I'm still hoarse. I was saying, with your being sick and all, I thought it my duty and obligation as a daughter, right? And I thought it was what Esteban and Sara expected of me. I'm not sure that you did, and frankly, I prefer not to second-guess you, but I think I'm right."

I now press my face against the mosquito netting and can see you breathing, just barely. You hardly have the strength to push up those big bones on your chest. Watching you, I can see how right I was in coming. I did want to see you. I hope it makes you happy to hear me say so, but I must confess to other reasons too, more selfish ones. I had to talk to you about me, and I feel compulsive about it. It's an old need I have. I hope you understand. I hear you sighing...a long, deep sigh. You're either exhausted or simply bored.

I'm sure you know the exact moment I set foot in your house. You always found out about everything even when I said nothing. In a voice which persists in coming out of me in small hushed tones, I repeat that Sara wrote me about your being sick. I don't know if I made it clear to you that the idea of coming was mine. I keep saying that you look well (I expected to find you in worse condition). How well I know that you can see through everything I say...you always did. You believe what you choose to and discard the rest. In any event I go on...

"You know how Sara is. Anything sends her into a

tizzy."

Sara thinks you may have little time left and I try to quiet her fears. She told me so in her letter and repeated it when she came and we were hugging one another. The poor girl...broke down in tears. She must really be frightened, she doesn't know if she can make it without you. You made a scarecrow out of her, Mother dear. She's little more than a puppet in your adroit hands. She is terrified now ... thinks the world will come to an end if you're not there. And since she's convinced that you haven't much time left, she thinks her time is up too, the silly girl. She went to pieces from the very first moment. But she'll survive. In any case, there's as much life left in you as you choose to have. You're not one to give up without a fight. You might have told that to my sister. You know how upset she becomes. But I didn't come here to argue with anybody. I'm going out for a while. I'd like to shower and change my clothes. I'm going to sit out on your balcony. It's a lovely night and I have lots to think about. I must prepare myself because we have to talk. Yes, there is a lot we have to say to one another, you and I. I will not leave until you hear me out, even if you limit yourself to just listening.

"**T**oday is now," I say to myself. I have this old habit of talking to myself as if I were two persons... the inside Mariana, and the outside one. "Get up!" I order myself. Obediently I put on my bathrobe and rummage through my bag for toothbrush, soapdish, and towel. I put the towel over my arm and leave the room. The air has warmed up and the bands of light through the window pane dazzle me. I reflect, "I do love this house." As I walk through it I fondle the smooth-polished cocoa-colored wood. The glu-glu of the water from the kitchen faucets reaches my ears. I realize that the woman who takes care of you has arrived, the one who looks after you when you nap and who indulges you like a child. I walk slowly toward the bathroom without her seeing me. I don't want her to see me this way, just out of bed, my hair messed up and without make-up. I wonder how she got into the house. She must have a key, is my response to myself. I dash into the bathroom without her noticing I passed in back of her. She is young and has a refreshing smell about her, something green-fresh. Is it a lemon smell? No. Fresh orange leaves? No. She smells of sandalwood. That's it! Bits and pieces of sandalwood!

I'm back here again. I explain some things to you inside of me as if you hear me talking to myself. I took great care in dressing up for you, using very little make-up. If you should decide to open your eyes I want to look as natural as possible.

"It's already today." I speak up now but not too loudly. I do not want to frighten you. "It's the morning I spoke about to you last night. Remember? Remember me? I was here beside you last night."

I advance slowly and discretely through the malodorous sheath of your illness. I see objects and details I hadn't noticed last night, an apparatus with an empty bag of serum hanging from a metal hook. Perhaps I hadn't noticed it because it was hidden behind the mosquito netting. I continue to look about in curiosity. There is ice and there are plastic cups, a blue box with a hypodermic syringe, a little bottle filled with reddish fluid, no doubt prescribed by the doctor, judging from the label, and a piece of rose-colored gingham folded over several times. I note that it is bulky but I resist my curiosity to discover its purpose and do not touch it. All of it invades your dressing table, everything is folded and part of you and your bed, which now is liberated from the white tent that covered you last night, in the oval mirror.

"I slept in the little bedroom off the balcony," I explain to you just as if you had asked. "The one that faces east. I have to admit that for a house in the country, it is beautiful. There is so much open space ... no accumulation of junk and useless knick-knacks which only provide a haven for dust, dust that chokes and gags the city housewife. Your house is not at all like that." Again, I say "your" house speaking simply and somewhat frivolously.

"I met the woman who keeps you company." I choose the words carefully. I could have said, the woman who takes care of you. "I like her, that one at least. I understand there are two of them."

This I say to you as I keep in mind that there are two. One because she is paid and the other because you were godmother to her youngest daughter at her confirmation. Sara told me all about it in her usual child-like expression of wonderment!

"You should have seen the people coming and going! Oh, Mariana, it was like a pilgrimage!"

"I like Berta," I comment so that you should know it was she whom I met.

I feel in some subtle way I'm beginning to pry into your affairs. I know how much it annoys you if I mix into your business, your life, your home, your people, your moods. This reiteration of the word "your" makes me think. Why do I constantly place it before everything connected with you? "I don't know," is the usual response of the other Mariana. (You know, the one I spoke of earlier.)

"It's good to have someone here with you" I whisper with a smile, making sure the silence in the room stretches no further.

I say nothing about how I envy your ability to win people over and how you shield yourself from loneliness. The solitude you have protected yourself from is insidious. I know it well! You have done well!

I return to my voiced "monologue" even though the absence of any movement on your part is so eloquent. It would not be of the slightest concern to you whether or not I slept well. I can't blame you . After all, you didn't invite me. Even if what I have to say is trivial to you, it is imperative for me...yes... "to break the ice" as my husband would have said. I should say, my "ex." Your indifference really doesn't matter. I did sleep well. Maybe it was the fresh air blowing in from the window, my weariness from the trip, or my seeing you

after so long an absence, or a combination of it all. I was
exhausted. I speak to you as if you really cared that I had no
nightmares and that I did not mind the silence of the night as
I conjured up throbbing lives invisibly surrounding me,
thousands of diminutive figures capable of crushing us all as
we sleep defenselessly.

But this isn't what I came to discuss with you, I caution
myself. I do not wish to reveal my feelings of persecution or
the terror I experience at being a single woman. I'm sick and
tired of your silence. I'd be better off if I continued to speak
to you inside myself, just as I do with my other me. You will
not daunt me. I know you're there hiding behind your lashes,
spying on me, hoping to get your strength back so you can get
up, rise from your ashes, be reborn... so that when you look
at me, you can reduce me to dust. Now, let's see... Like before.
I have my doubts, but I won't know until... no... you're
moving! A barely perceptible "ay" escapes your lips. I approach you, then I hear Berta's voice. She is standing in the
doorway saying, "There she's goin' on back again." She
appears to be chanting, and dragging out her syllables.

I am full of curiosity.

"Does she sleep all the time?"

Without so much as a glance at me (according to her
norms of conduct, it would be a lack of respect), she explains
how Mama dozes on and off.

"When she complains a lot, I give her a little "*frotito.*"

She turns and points to a jar of roots and dry leaves. I
gather that the "*frotito*" is a massage. She continues to speak
in her crooning honey-comb voice. "Sometimes she has a bad
bellyache. It makes me feel bad..."

She shows me a poultice made of crude-looking
leaves of sage and mugwart pressed into a piece of rose-

colored gingham. She solemnly explains how she warms it before placing it at the hollow of your stomach.

"I heat it up in this little black pot," she smiles as she points to a pot from which smoke is rising." I heat the water in it then I dip the rag in and wring it out. It comes out nice and hot," she repeats as she looks into my eyes. Then she continues:"Lamamamialiuntamantecaeculebra" (Mamamiadearestcuresalwithsnakeoil). Quickly she loosens the mosquito netting, rolls it up and hangs it over the two nails on the wall. Her hands are now at rest and she looks up at me.

"If not that, I use grease," she concludes.

I look at her in puzzlement since I do not understand what she is saying. I ask and she explains patiently that she uses chicken fat...

"Fat," she repeats, possibly because she is amazed at my ignorance.

I step aside because she is busy running around arranging your toilette.

"I wonder what time it is?" She is thinking to herself rather than asking me and is looking out the window.

"Twelve after ten," I inform her knowing she hasn't asked me but must have noticed I have a watch.

"Then it's time for the bath," she reassures herself as if she had asked herself the question.

She already has everything organized. She approaches you calling: "*Viejita*! Come, dear!"

She handles you as if you might break and I make my escape. I flee because the thought of witnessing the devastation of your intimacy frightens me. I suspect that pity dictates that I not be abashed at your feelings of shame.

I take refuge on your balcony with a book Antonio has lent me. I obstinately persist in thinking in terms of the familiar "you" and in talking with you inside myself as if you can hear me. I figure it's all the same whether you hear me or not. You are not about to argue. My opening up to you is like extracting deep-seated memories from within, even if I am diffusing them inside myself. At this point I feel lost because I am uncertain of my logic. But I won't chew it over again. I feel a compulsion to verbalize everything for you. Each and every sentiment has a name which identifies it and I intend to dig it all out from wherever it may be interred...that's it...disinter things, play around with them, if you so permit...let them blow in the wind. I don't care if you think it stupid. I already know you do! You will think me hopelessly illogical to insist on tormenting myself with bitter memories among which you are always the most bitter. If I were able to feel some hint of happiness, true happiness, this would be a real occasion for celebration...and do you know why? I just said your opinion doesn't matter a bit to me. Take note!

On this sunny morning even the butterflies are flying about madly. You should not be surprised by my susceptibility to magic and my tendency to rant and rave.

A honeyed ululating song reaches my ears and I identify it at once. It is your neighbor, the little mother, still a child. She is rocking her baby. The innocent is cradled on its mother's full breasts, the breasts of a new mother. I see her from in-between the wooden slats of your balcony...a child-mother...singing. I try to guess her age...fifteen perhaps, or maybe less. It grieves me that her adolescence has been sacrificed by the transformation to motherhood. She sings:

Arro-rro, arro-rro, sleep baby sleep
Arro-rro, arro-rro, sleep my sun, my son
Arro-rro, arro-rro, sleep heart of hearts

The two of them, mother and babe, rock back and forth in the rocking chair to the song. I barely hear her and when I do, I'm tempted to cover my ears but I can't keep the song from reaching them. Thus the morning passes mindlessly for me in the company of the book and the rocking chair. I can't understand why they built her house here, stuck up as it is against the barbed wire that cordons off your property. But there it is and because of it, her life interlaces with my book.

Berta has come in to ask if I want lunch.

"I fixed a dish of codfish and tomatoes for you, *una viandita*," she announces as she struts about, her smile as provocative as the twinkle in her eye.

I figure she has fried the cod and tomatoes in achiote oil with garlic and the thought of it whets my appetite.

"If you like, I'll bring it to you," she drones on, tilting her head with a smile on her face which strikes me as a bit impish.

I smile and refuse her offer. Unexpectedly I ask: "What did she have to eat?"

"A couple of sips of milk with mint." She sighs disapprovingly. "She takes some chicken soup in the afternoon. *Don* Esteban usually brings home some good fat chickens for the soup."

Then I recall that Esteban had already left for the chicken farm when I woke up. I will see him this afternoon and we're having supper together. Then what will we do? Talk about the past? Watch a movie on TV or maybe spend time in the room where you are suffering death throes from an illness which makes losers of us all? Actually I don't care. Whatever we do, I'll be happy to be with him. With this thought in mind I'm quite content to follow Berta into the kitchen and I sit down after washing my hands. I like watching her as she moves about. I admire the diligence she displays in every-thing she does. She scrubs the pots and pans and piles them up on the rack. She washes the plate she ate lunch from and returns it to the cupboard above the kitchen sink. Then as I watch, she moves to the ice chest to remove the chicken she had mentioned.

"This woman, this native woman is a diamond in the rough," I say to my inner Mariana who is quick to respond. "I would certainly say she is a jewel."

I confess I would covet her for myself.

I've been sitting at your side for an hour and I still don't know whether you know I'm here. I hope in vain that you will open your eyes and look at me. Berta tells me you were up when I was resting.

"Just a little bit," she points out referring to your brief arousal. Since it's possible that you will open your eyes for another little bit, I settle into your easy chair, your grand-daughter's gift to you, and I wait patiently. Why not use this time to tell you what I came to say.

I feel you resent me somewhere in your subconscious. I am the scorpion of a thousand legs, for you, a venomous snake. You imagine me scratching around, a female mouse, searching for a place into which I can sink my rodent-like teeth. You listen to me moving around, listen to me pulling at the spider webs in the corners of your house, and you lock yourself in. You do not wish to see your remorse in my torment. No matter! Now it's me who doesn't want you looking for me! It's enough that you are listening to me through the stench of your illness and your obstinate silence. As I said, it really doesn't matter! I wasn't expecting a brass band or a banquet. I came for peace of mind and for you to let me into the no-man's land of no love and my bitterness. Let me go! Cut the apron strings! I want to be myself! Me! With my own bones, my own tongue, like fresh running water! If only I could break the barriers that hold back stagnant waters and let them pour out! This has to catch your attention. You who are so prudent, so measured. And why not? It's always the same! Though it may seem like subterfuge to you, you must be aware that I don't enjoy using hurtful words; it's not in my character. When I tell you to let me go, I'm aware that it is a contradiction. How can you break the ties when they are not coming from you to me but the other way around, making me responsible for binding us together. If you were lucid enough to understand what I am saying in such a roundabout way, you would look at me with those beautiful steel-grey eyes and smile your delicate probing smile. You would say everything without uttering a single word. There was never any room for weakness or pettiness in you. You would put up or shut up and that was that. Everything resolved... I'm leaving now for just a few minutes for a breath of fresh air outside of your room. I'll be back later. I'm still hoping that during one of your escapes or returns from or to this world, you may become aware of my presence. Before I leave I want to make one thing clear: the word remorse; it doesn't become you.

I hide in a corner to escape the women who have come to pay their respects...the pilgrimage, as Sara would put it. It makes me squirm to be the unconcerned daughter, the one who lives far away and who couldn't care less if Godmother Ernestina lives or dies. I flee from their curiosity and judgment. "Why?" I ask myself. "Because you're weak." An interjected judgment from my inner twin.

Agueda, the woman who looks after you when you are napping and who spoils you, enters. Berta, standing next to her, sings out:

"So you must be Agueda, the woman who stays with *Doña* Ernestina when I'm not here."

She departs, leaving her duties in other hands.

I note that I am indulging in the same habit of talking to you even when we are not face-to-face. I hate admitting it, but it's a habit born of loneliness. I am used to talking with my mouth closed. Agueda sits down beside me on the bench. I do not blame her for not attending to you. Like me, she is escaping from the town gossips.

"They are reciting the rosary," she states simply.

I look at her and though I ask nothing, she clarifies: "We here, all belong to the Church of Our Lord..."

"But maybe not all of us." I think, somewhat astonished. She then says as if she were reading my mind:

"Then Halleluya, as they say around here."

Her candor delights me. I flash her an understanding smile which she returns.

On impulse, I find myself looking for the page in the book where I left off reading, but I feel it would be a discourtesy Agueda does not deserve. I close the book knowing I entered a marvelous kingdom of another world to bear witness to the supremely fascinating transformation of MacKendal. It would have been much better than hearing what Agueda has to say.

"That silly little ninny had a baby girl," she says, lowering her voice as if fearing to be overheard.

I maintain my silence but she insists on my knowing. More to please her than anything else, I search my memory for the silly ninny. I can think of no one and I do not wish to appear disinterested. I keep my head up and try to look alert. I ask no questions because I do not want to know. Agueda cannot understand my silence.

"The little ninny, the one from Nicanor..." she persists pointing with her very long fingernail to the house on the hill.

"Country bumpkin," snorts my other Mariana sarcastically. Agueda doesn't deserve this.

I turn away because it isn't my place to pass judgment. After all it's not her fault. What has she got to do with changing customs in the hill country?

"The government built that house for her," Agueda explains.

I have no choice. I look at the house if only out of curiosity to see what it's like. It might have been built with the hands and sweat of the owner as in the past, just as my father built his, and his father before him. However for Agueda the most important thing is not that the mayor comes around passing out houses for the peasants to satisfy the politics of the moment, but that I capture a sense of the environment, to orientate myself to the morbid, unhealthy atmosphere of what goes on inside. I am an unwilling observer. I look on and she no longer hesitates:

"Her grandfather did it to her," she stares at me, waiting for a reaction.

I have to ask what it was he did to her because I can no longer remain at the margin of pain which I would not like to add to my own. She continues in an outraged tone:

"The little girl...the grandfather did it to her," she explains so I can become as shocked as she is.

I can no longer control my feelings now and I ask: "Why didn't someone stop him? Why didn't anyone protect her?" I finish angrily.

"It happened when Jesusa, a member of the family, had to go into town on business. The boys were at school and another member of the family was traveling in the area. The old man took advantage." She shrugs her shoulders. "He probably got all hot and bothered when he saw her taking off her clothes, when he saw her naked flesh. Men carry Satan around inside of them, *Doña* Mariana."

"His grand-daughter, Mariana! How horrible!"

Then I cried, though the tears did not flow outside. I cried in bewilderment and fear. I cried inside myself.

I feel a resurgence of profound bitterness. The vision of opaque yellow eyes spying with lust on the innocent child makes my flesh crawl. Lizard, snake, scorpion! I curse in fury under my breath. Nausea floods my insides when I remember violence like that in Arturo's arms what seems like a million years ago. "The first times were the best..." I reflect when memory hits me like a slap in the face. It emerges wrapped in spider webs dragged along in a confusion of subterfuge and deception, and installs itself perversely on the balcony. My tacit complicity! My pleasure and my shame! in allowing you to play with my body in the dark silence of my room. "Open your portals, Mariana, your arms, your legs...open your house." You ruined so much of my life to satisfy your appetites!

"But if I remember correctly..." intercepts my other voice.

"Did I accept it with pleasure?" I ask, wounded by her tone. Yes! "With pleasure and joy! What woman doesn't at first?"

"Then, why?" She insists on pressing the misery of my humiliation and my unhappy memory."

"How do I know?" "Maybe it was because I was in love, because I wanted to please him, or I was naive."

"How many reasons one can give for submitting!"

Down below among the yagrumo trees, a rare species of bird is rasping out its song..."cu-ju, cu-ju cu-ju." Blue flies buzz overhead and down among the trees. The rare bird, the poor creature, is choking out his song and I choke too thinking about poor little Inés. I remember her now. She's the child who always cried when she wanted something because she didn't know how to speak.

"I saw her eight years ago when I was here last," I tell Agueda. "They weren't living over here then, but over there. They were farm hands."

She nods in assent and is surely lost in thought. My head fills with a single vision, that of a lily-white face encircled by a dainty white ruffle. The small white body is bearing the weight of an old slimy one who is penetrating her rose-apple flesh, spilling its depraved juices and stinking like an old toad over her virgin thighs. Lord Almighty, what a heinous crime! I cannot help visualizing it, inventing details. I imagine him watching her in the night, listening in stealth for the quiet rhythmic breathing of others before making his move. A serpent, a spider, a venomous snake dragging along on reptile feet, barefoot, of course, so that she can't hear him. I see the old lizard hand closing over the carnation of Spain, the small rosy mouth, to quell her protestations, to calm her fears...to keep her from crying out, screaming. I can imagine his hoarse whisper:

"It's only me, your grandfather," into her tender ear, and she silent and drowsy. "It's me, my little dove."

His hand, dirtier than the dung heap on Esteban's farm, runs over her. My flesh crawls when I think of his stinking mouth over the sweet fragrant cupped carnation of her mouth, in a gluttonous kiss. I experience all these thoughts in a matter of seconds and am about to vomit.

Agueda notices that the women are done with their prayers.

"I'll serve some refreshments," she says as she stands up from the bench.

I can't allow her to go without telling me whether or not the man was punished. Whatever they might have done to him wouldn't be enough. Never, Never could it match the magnitude of the crime.

"Wasn't he sentenced?"

Agueda looks at me, incredulous.

"No. Her godmother wanted them to operate, but the doctor wouldn't do it."

I was disconcerted by the tone of her response. It was as if she approved. "Why, oh why, Lord?" I asked in desperation. "Aren't there enough wrinkled blue babies born from fathers, brothers, or a beast of a grandfather? That bunch of snakes! I hate them all!"

"And me, I hate them too," snaps my other voice. Sometimes it agrees with me.

"I'm back again," I whisper softly so that you don't detect the hoarseness of my voice. "I've been here several times already but for all practical purposes, you weren't really here. What I mean to say is that you were asleep or going back again, as Berta says. Esteban came too with his dog Gringo, Esteban grinning his customary mischievous, little boy grin. He came up very concerned about you. That should make you feel good.

"Should I be worried too?" I ask my other voice as I walk over to the armchair. She suggests that perhaps I'm not, because I know your capacity for incredible resistance. Her reasoning is a relief. I am unable to endure feelings of guilt and I always get hurt in these situations.

As I watch you sleep, I think about Esteban. He looks old and worn-out to me. I don't know. It is more than physical exhaustion. It was confirmed last night when he told me something I found hard to understand.

"The doctor is coming tomorrow."

"Why isn't she in the hospital?" He remains thoughtful for a few moments.

"Because she wasn't getting the proper care. She was already in The Regional when she had her attack. Everything was fine in Intensive Care. She evidently did not know what was going on. When she left that unit, she complained about everything...the nurses, the service.. everything. So I arranged to bring her home." He says home, not her house or the house...a detail I pick up on, analyze and instantly approve.

"Is it normal for her to sleep so much?" I ask in a loud and clear voice, like his, so that if you're listening, you know what we're discussing.

"Well..." he begins, biting on his lower lip as he searches for an appropriate way of saying something difficult. I wait patiently. "I asked the doctor to prescribe sedatives for her," he concludes lowering his voice at last as if inviting me to join the complicity.

"Sedatives?" I repeat in the same tone. "Why? Isn't it better for her to sit up, to remain alert, to talk?"

He opens his huge round eyes.

"She doesn't accept her condition. The day she came home, she tried getting up by herself, to go out to the balcony. I was feeding the chickens down below. Agueda's shouts sent me flying upstairs. Mama had suffered a dizzy spell and I found her on the floor. Poor Agueda hadn't the strength to lift her. She has only come to herself the last couple of days," he explains, a bit more relaxed now. I feel he is offering me an apology and I smile tenderly at him.

"I'm not really in a hurry to leave," I tell him. "I do have a doctor's appointment but I can go and come back soon."

I am actually relieved because I know now your silence is not entirely born of willfulness.

It is after eleven and Esteban still does not turn off the light in your room. Suddenly I notice you moving. You open your eyes, flutter your eyelids and call softly: "Esteban." I approach you.

"What is it?" equally softly.

"Could you help me?" The request is stated faintly but clearly.

"Help you? How?" I mix tenderness with resentment.

"He knows..." she whispers without hesitation.

I call him and he hurries in saying:

"Time for your medicine."

"Stupid of me not to think of it!" I reproach myself, distressed. I hold up the spoon with the red liquid as you raise your head so that you do not choke when you swallow. You grimace and I take note of the way you look.

"Would you like some water?" I ask you. You respond with a tenuous smile. If you want it, you want him to give it to you.

I draw back without resentment. I realize that the years do not pass without consequences. After quenching your thirst, it is clear you wish to retreat again. I lower my voice and say to Esteban:

"It's so late and you're still not in bed."

"I read a lot and she's always calling me."

"Why does she always call you?"

" I really don't know," he whispers thoughtfully.

"I do know, I think. My dear mother is finally becoming human; she's finally asking for help. Why does she call so often?"

"She almost always wants water."

The good-natured smile that spreads across his face reveals your status as his spoiled darling.

Now that he has left the room, I sit down quietly again in the black and white chair. I no longer feel the bitterness I spoke of before. "Don't go looking for it again, Mariana," my friendly inner voice counsels, the voice of my twin. Well then, if that's the way it is, I will! The fact is you wake me up with a clear head making demands, no matter what time of the day or night it is, sedatives or no sedatives! You do ask for water whether you need it or not, to satisfy a thirst that doesn't exist!

He is your water, your well, your fountain. Now I see through your silence which I know represents the obedient child of your will. You enter and leave, come and go as you wish, and see those you wish to see. It is only me you deny! You cast me out! Correction! You abandoned us! The tortured look on Sara's face shows that you still revel in making her unhappy. Want to know something? You're wasting your time playing cat and mouse with me. Remember it's not for naught that I am your work of art. Anyhow, I'm an old cat too. That's why I know you're listening. I know that you've watched me prying, pensive, and bleeding since I've arrived. You heard me come in, heard me calling you so tenderly: Mama, Mamita! There it was...my voice, controlled and indulging you, pampering and cajoling you with those names. It really wasn't me, the real me! It was a mask, one I use every day as a cover. I kid you not. I want us both to be clear about this, and forgive me for calling a spade a spade. My instinct for self-preservation keeps me from letting you see the real me. You would destroy her in one fell swoop, with one single gesture, one look of total indifference. Yes, you would bleed me white, make me into a painted bird, a green lemon. You would tear the petals from my flower.

    I get up on this second day in your house and go to see whether you're awake. I approach your bed, barefoot to prevent the slightest noise. I part the curtain of the mosquito netting to look at you. You are also looking at me. You see me through a gray veil, like a mist which covers your pupils. I find no expression in your eyes. I guess you can see me only in shadow-mist, a swept-up spider web, across the small space that separates us. I call you by the name I always used as a child: "Mamita... Mama Ernestina. Do you recognize me?"

    I wait for what seems an eternity until I hear your

feeble voice.

"Y...Yes."

I try again: "Who am I?" This time your whisper comes more quickly:

"Sara."

I rebel. Is this possible? What is this? I can't believe it! I say this to myself in exasperation. My other self banters:

"Neither can I."

"You infuriate me, don't you know that?" I rant and rave at her in silence and she suavely responds, egging me on:

"And you me."

Berta arrives at seven. I try to look concerned. Maybe I really am, without even realizing it. I inform her that you didn't sleep well during the night and that I tried to give you the aspirin. I show her the cup of milk with the dissolved aspirin. She smiles exposing her large teeth, big black and white choppers stained by nicotine. Then she says:

"Don't worry. We'll give them to her with breakfast." Her churning sing-song makes me realize how little I know about the folks living on the hill. Berta talks that way, distorting vowels and mixing syllables Her chatter sounds like musical bird-talk.

I hear her fixing coffee in the kitchen. The fragrance comes to me along with constant mutterings through the bathroom door. She plans her day aloud as she beats the boiled milk with a black coconut shell. After a while she calls out:

"Come in, *Doña* Marianita, come have your coffee."

I hear Esteban talking to the dog and I hurry to join him for breakfast.

"Here, take it," Berta urges me as she places a cup painted with little blue flowers before me.

Esteban pushes the sugar bowl over to me as I spread butter on the biscuits Berta has placed on the table. I notice that she addresses me with familiarity and I like it.

Esteban has already left. We said good-bye to each other after breakfast, on your balcony. He asked about my plans for the day and I about his, no formalities nor amenities. Outside the fields smell of wet grass. I resist the temptation for a walk because my room is not yet tidied and I want to at least make the bed before Berta comes up. I can hear her moving around from here.

"You're having a bath today," she tells you matter-of-factly, and without hesitation as she moves around to coordinate her movements over you with the towel.

"Stupid, dumbbell," I hear you protesting in your wasted old voice.

How can you? I am indignant, but Berta clearly pays you no mind. She changes your nightgown and I hear her say:

"Put your hand here... here... here," she repeats with saintly patience.

Ah Ha! She is very chummy with you too. Don't ask me why, but I am certain that the familiarity has another ring when it applies to me. You are our awesome version of the terrible *Doña* Bárbara from the Venezuelan plains of Rómulo who has been transformed into the soft, flabby rag doll, disheveled and trembling in her strong, fine hands, peasant hands from atop the mountain, where you built your house with a strong eagle eye in order to dominate imperiously.

I hear her sing. The song is almost a prayer; it is soft in tone and reaches me. She is lulling you to sleep with a lullaby, crooning you to sleep.

A wreck, a tattered doll, a child, a nursing baby, slipping away day by day. If you don't get up and move soon, you'll be back in your fetal state. May I ask a question? I know, it's not possible to make this kind of choice, but if you could return to your fetal state and had the power to choose, would you choose as your mother the possesser of the voice now crooning over you? I think you would, I do. You wouldn't at all mind a little runt sperm creeping up her uterine wall, entering her body. You would curl up in a ball and without any thought or emotion you would be transformed into a seed and covered by a membrane of skin and cartilage and on the day of your birth be discharged from the uterine opening. Happy indeed you would be to exchange your balding old mother for this young one, certainly more of a mother than either you or I.

Yes Ma'am, I believe you would have it so! You would take my dear old granny away from me with pleasure, without the slightest compunction, knowing that her small, white, twisted, dried-out body is all that's left of her for me. You always resented your mother. I was never able to understand why. It showed in your voice when you spoke to her. You turned to stone. Fortunately the old lady was protected by our love, so she was not wounded by your resentment. She had so many loves, so many! A speck of cotton, the little head of a bird, a humming bird, muncher of flowers and balsam apples.

The warmth of grandmother's skirt still takes the chill from me as I recall how my silly little finger searched for sleep in my mouth. Happy and drowsy I sucked on it over her starched skirt as her hand traveled up and down my back sometimes stopping at my little back-end, and then, smack, smack a few small pats and up it went again. Her voice was not so old or cracked that it couldn't pour tenderness over my bobbing butterfly head as I rested on her lap. I remember my dreams, her song, her green-wood fragrance and her hard, gentle hands. Lost, running through the mountains with me; chasing marvelous birds determined to hide; chirping, hidden in the branches, the leaves and the dark green roof. Her voice, her hands and I, yearning to know the meaning of the songs and the voices in the yellow wind and whispering leaf storm.

I go back in time and again I am her little mischievous martinet, bathing in the clear warm rough water in knickers made from burlap rice sacks and she in her shepherd's pants made of the same material. I remember the *soponcitos* of purple bananas and the *guineos mafafos* toasted and roasted around the camp fire of packed-down earth, the sweet rice, the pines, the wild red juicy strawberries and sour soup. She, the wind and the sky...and the clouds flying madly about. I, the busy little bee intent on sucking all the honey out of the country which was part of my grandmother and my hardy loquacious uncles. Wishing I were a branch, a leaf, a bird, a cloud. To see everything. To know everything. To share the laughter of the leaves and the wind, the whisperings of turtledoves and mozambiques. To penetrate the mystery. To expose the sharp, green world, fragrant with resin and raining white drizzle over the tender grass, for me, for my eyes, for my hands. For me to be one—one—one—with it all. With every-thing! Everything! Everything!

"Do you know that I'm an uprooted person," I say to you from the black and white armchair." I go around looking for somewhere to set down roots. Now after all my struggles, I've given up. I'm more flexible when I have to be. At least I'm trying. What do you want? It's hard to teach an old dog new tricks! As I was saying, I'm giving in. Remember how stubborn I was? The old Mariana, the one who never gave up on her ideas? Unhappily and worst of all how incredibly hard-headed I was in agreeing to marry Arturo. Please don't get me wrong, I'm not complaining. My marriage was the worst mistake of my life. Arturo never wanted me. Why should I deny it now? Since then a lot of water has passed under the bridge and the truth is that I have to talk to you openly, with my heart on my sleeve, I no longer care, I've had my Via Crucis, I sure did. He took me, deflowered me and used me from the start. My flesh became covered with thorns, my tongue became crude and dirty and my words like stiff broom whisks. Pure broom whisks. I embitter the air I breathe and it embitters me. Bitterness is distilled throughout the house. It isn't easy to speak of certain things but since I'm opening up I can tell you that my life as a married woman—at least since your grand-daughter was born—has been a nightmare of licentious dreams in the bedroom of a single woman. A room without the smell of a man. Seven days and seven nights, and only one of the seven, the odor of a male goat came to me. The conscientious husband! The one who fulfills obligations I never imagined would disgust me so much! An entire bar of soap wasn't enough! All the water in the world couldn't remove the rotten, pervasive, alien stink which it was my duty to endure each Sunday morning.

Now what have you got to say about my miseries? Haven't you anything to say? Nothing? Oh, I see. You'd rather hide what you have to say under that impassive mask. You don't want to get into it. Well, O.K. Hide in silence if it makes you happy and I'll go back to mine...

But I hear something coming from you. I swear I heard you: "What did you expect, Mariana, that you had the right to receive and not give back?" But what do you know about it, miser, about what it is to give? Tell me, you dried-out little raisin, you wrinkled prune, shell of a seed? How do you know what it means to give until there is nothing left? To give without anyone's acceptance or appreciation of anything you do, because everyone thinks you are insensitive, egocentric and hard...and no one knows that it was you who left me this legacy, this obvious lack of feeling...a Johnson's powder little white roach, if you like, or - to give you the benefit of the doubt - if you could open your eyes and speak, you would say: "Go back to where you came from. I have problems enough of my own."

You are right. This is not the time nor the place. But I must vent my spleen. I will not bear this burden for the rest of my life. You caused me pain and I feel compelled to douse you with some of it... If I don't, I'll never be able to fill the vacuum with things that may be coming my way, perhaps at this very moment.

I must be in control of my sanity and serenity, and have them become part of me or I might lose out. And so, little grit of an antique clock, grit which is running out, hiding or not, I'm not about to leave you in peace. Pretend you're sleeping, if you like. But no, my dear, I'm not leaving you.

The rasping of the small bird reaches me through the open window, the same bird that rasped away yesterday among the yagrumo trees. My heart weeps for him. I approach you and touch you. I run my hand over your dry crepe-paper skin. Mindlessly I pinch the loose skin on your stick-like arm, between my fingers. I feel an enormous impulse to scream. Before I run out, I ask Berta to call me when you "wake up."

I'm not certain how long I've been here, seated on the steps of "your" stairwell in "your" house. "Now we're chummy and personal again," the second Mariana mocks maliciously. Sometimes I think she is number one girl, because I pay so much attention to her and her opinions. This moment now belongs to me and I'll ignore her. I have no time for her. My drooping eyes are closing. The heat has become more intense. I can almost press it up against me like a sheet of heavy air. I listen for any sound as I probe and penetrate the silence. I discover a new whisper, a gentle one, close to me. When I open my eyes, I see the leaves of the white oak and the mimosa swaying quietly. The whisper is almost without sound: it is small and close, and not from leaf to leaf. I think it is a playful breeze which has settled in among the silent branches as I fantasize. It moves them closer together, ever gentle as it frolics about playfully.

Above on the slope the sun has broken up into pieces. There are a few dark pools, dark brown shadows on the mountain-side. The defiant female shadow is becoming darker, more resolute. "Sun, do not penetrate me," I imagine it to say. Master of the chicken coop, wild steed, sparrow hawk. I defy and challenge you. I, a little crumbling fresh water cloud... me, I challenge you. I'm not afraid of you."

The plaint of a dove from a nearby place lures me.

"It's a lonely little *macho*," says Berta over my shoulder as she probes the sky apprehensively. "It looks like there's time." She chants without taking her eyes off the dark clouds.

"A storm with this kind of sun!" I'm shocked into silence. We again hear the "currucu cu currucu" from the solitary bird.

"It's a little ringed male, a *collarín*," says Berta as she listens and turns to look at the trees, perhaps trying to locate the dove.

"He doesn't know how to live alone either," I think. "Only the dead do."

Something breaks the silence of "your" house. Maybe it's coming from "your" room. Perhaps you are coming to look for yourself, child, in "your" field of anemones and wild daisies and you are complaining because you cannot find yourself. Are you complaining? I don't know. I don't even know if you are you. The now you. Or the child inside of which I still not am. The air is strangely still. Everything seems to be at an impasse. The oak branches and the mimosa barely tremble. Berta is still behind me sniffing the air like a dog. She breathes deeply as if searching for scents. I know this because I can hear her sipping in the air. Below in a fenced-in area, a black bull is bellowing. Esteban says he is the toughest of his bulls. "He is a stud, a breeding bull," he has told me with pride.

"Aren't they all?" my other Mariana whispers in an attempt to ingratiate herself with me.

"But of course," I admit more out of charity than anything else.

Berta comments over my shoulder:

"I heard a guinea hen singing at the stroke of twelve yesterday."

And just as if it were overheard, one of your hens clucks: "choclo, choclo, choclo. Bearer of evil omen! I ponder angrily. "Messenger of farewells, soothsayer," I turn and look at Berta.

"Calling for rain...?

She almost looks my way, but no, her eyes avoid me.

"I really don't know," she says thoughtfully," but last night the dogs were howling too. Probably some Christian soul who..."

The suspense says it all. How little she knows you! She thinks you are dying. I know that you're not. I don't doubt you've had a look at the other world, maybe you have been touched by it, but you are still not prepared to surrender yourself. You are obstinate, tenacious, and tough, a wild mountain goat. I know you well. If you face death as you did life, no pain, no gain in it.

I tarry a bit longer on your stairwell. The sun is hitting on your steps, I think, using the language I hear from Berta. It almost licks my feet. When it reaches my knees, I will leave, because my head is resting on them. Inside the house the "chaqui, chaqui" sound of Berta's slippers reaches my ears. I follow her around in my head. She comes and goes rapidly. She uncovers a pot, then I hear the noise of the lid as it is transferred to another pot or casserole, the sound of metal. Now, she opens the ice chest; a brief silence and she closes it. She is moving around again, "chaqui, chaqui." Soon she will call me to lunch. What has she prepared today? I dream about it until I hear her call.

"Mariana," she yells as if I were a thousand miles away. "Time for lunch!"

"*Vianda*, cod fish and tomatoes, no doubt! Daily peasant fare and exquisite fare for city folk. My other idiot self comments that peasants aren't the rustics they used to be and would resent being called to table in this manner.

"But they are peasants," I answer with impatience, in that they are simple, down-to-earth people who are obliging and wholesome."

My mind turns to lunch again. I'd love some guinea hen with eggplant and codfish—or some corn fritters, I'm thinking as I rise to go to the table. Berta is busy cutting my lunch into little pieces. She says nothing, but her motherly smile reveals her concern for the devastating effects my illness has wrought on my hands.

"How good this sweet potato tastes!" I exclaim after the first bite. "Aren't you eating.?"

"Ummmm," she mutters with a playful smile. "Woman eating more and more...Gets belly she's not looking for." "But not you, you have no belly."

"Who has a belly? I'm just a hank of hair and a hunk of bone...and I wear a girdle," I confess.

"Always?"

"Almost always." I smile at her.

"Listen up. I'm going to tell you something. Listen to this. You know, when those pants came out, the Levis, I mean, I told Cajlito (I presume Carlito is her husband) I said to him I would buy me a pair. OK? , right?...O.K.? So I bought me a pair of them and couldn't get them on. So I decided to get me one of those girdles and then try to squeeze into them. How else was I going to fit this big, fat ass of mine in? I went and bought the thing and almost choked myself to death. It nearly strangled me. I couldn't breathe. So...the Hell with it! I pulled it off. Bye-bye girdle! To the "dron!" Squeeze someone else's damn ass!

I deduced that the "dron" must be the basket of dirty

wash.

"You just have to get used to it." I say to encourage her to continue speaking her pidgin lingo. I think about it for a moment and she shakes her head in approval.

"Yup, that's it! It's getting used to it. But it made me real mad. Your mama," she said becoming grave in tone, "When she first came here, she was using the thing and these 'bristas' came out of her" (I translate once again, "blisters") "the awful kind, the kind that peels. She couldn't reach her back, because they came out over here," and she turns to show me, touching herself with her open hand—"higher than the last bone in the back. So your Mama found a salve in town that you could smear on."

Here I have to make an effort and I deduce that they resorted to First Aid in the city, the American cure-all.

Now I hear one of your soft moans. I hear it from the bed where I have been trying to catch forty winks, just as you have...without any luck.

"It looks like Berta has already left," I say to myself because I cannot feel her presence anywhere.

"She did not leave," Mariana informs me from her domain. "She left after she picked some flowers from the oak tree."

Boiled oak flowers, Berta's loving attempt to smooth and make fragrant your iguana-like skin, I reflect, of course with you in mind. And again, butting in as usual, the other Mariana: "Just like yours." And she is right. I observe my arms and run my deformed hands over them. Then I cross them and hug my shoulders. I am embracing myself! My God! I'm hugging myself!

I hear you groaning again. "Ay!" This time it doesn't sound weak, it is not a cry of pain. It is an angry shout. "Idiot! Stupid!"

Oh, Ho! There you are! You see?! You are there for those you want to see! I knew it! Agueda's voice is trying to calm you down.

"Shh...easy...easy," she murmurs gently. "I'm trying to change you before I give you the rice. See? Rice with curdled milk just what you like, *comadre*."

I remember now that you are not wearing your false teeth. You interrupt again saying: "Stupid idiot, you're digging your nails into me!" You repeat this in an even more furious voice, like an ill-tempered parrot. "Beast! You animal!"

I don't believe Agueda is mistreating you, but I investigate all the same. I've given up on napping. Besides, I owe it to you to be concerned about you. She is changing the urine-soaked cloth under your wrinkled buttocks. The rice and milk are waiting for you on the dressing table which was once mine. Remember? How could you forget? You grumble just as if you can read my mind.

Yes; who can forget it? It was part of the war of nerves we two sustain. I have asked myself so many times why it would be so difficult for me to accept your hospitality. You did help us when we needed it most...when Arturo lost his job and I was suffering the horrors of morning sickness with my first pregnancy. Arturo said we were lucky to have you with us and he was right. But I didn't feel lucky. I felt humiliated and ashamed to live off your charity. But I have to thank you for never reproaching me for my ever present black moods. They made our lives so difficult! How my ingratitude must have offended you!

Why didn't you ever say anything or try to understand my hostility? You are my mother. I should have loved you, showed you affection, respect, at least, consideration. Weren't you at all curious to find out why I acted as I did? How different our relationship might have been if you had asked me!

Always, from the day you left me with Papa, I longed to be back with you. There I was, suddenly, without you. It was painful to be in your house, feeling rejected as I did. My bones told me that your generosity did not come from your heart. I so wanted to convince myself that it did. It would have made me happy to know that you hadn't acted out of charitable impulse or some misguided notion of filial devotion.

I do not really want to hurt you but out of curiosity, could you tell me if you were ever serious about keeping us at home with you as part of your world, part of your life, close to you? I don't believe so. I have no desire to bother you now, but as far as you were concerned, we were merely guests, visitors. At least, that was my impression. We were birds in flight, Mama Ernestina, migratory birds!

I recall that when either of us left the house, I always asked for your blessing. It was by force of habit, and you always responded in the same way. "God bless you, child," but it never came from the heart. I was able to perceive your indifference just as you could my rancor. But that was so long ago. That old custom is gone now and who wants to dig up old ghosts?

I compare Berta and Agueda in my head. Berta, who always whispered softly in your ear: "Some oatmeal dear? Oh, my pretty old dear! Eat up or I'll eat it," threatening you as she would a naughty child. Not Agueda. She would be serious and measured in her approach. "You must eat because the doctor is coming today. Do you want him to give you another injection? No? Well, good! Now, eat up!"

Tired of standing in the doorway observing the scene, I enter smiling at Agueda.

"How are things this afternoon?" I inject a false note of levity to ease the situation, to make Agueda feel more at ease as she takes care of you.

Then you smile at me and any hypocritical intent that might have existed in my greeting is obliterated. There is real joy now.

"How are you?" I ask gently.

You should not suspect by the tone of my voice that I know that you have been ignoring me. Nor do I ask you if you know who I am, because we both know that you know. Now, my dear mother, you are awake, you are lucid, and scratching about.

I nestle comfortably into Teresa's small armchair and enjoy watching Agueda arrange the pillows behind your head. She then tucks a towel under your chin in a barber-like swoop and casts a glance at the plate of rice and milk on the dresser.

"Leave me alone," you grumble sullenly.

Surprise of surprises! Agueda pays no attention to you, doesn't even listen to you! How does she dare ignore you? You, the one who always gave orders and who had the last word! Amazing! I never in my wildest dreams thought you could be overruled. How is it that you permit this relaxation of your authority? Don't tell me! Let me guess! You're beginning to come off your high horse!

Agueda turns her head toward me as you eat; she lowers her voice as if in complicity, and remarks:

"I think she's dying..."

I look at her, startled. She twists her mouth in the direction of the window.

"The little baby girl," she whispers in an attempt to hide the painful news from your ears. "They were up all night with her," she continues and she adds in the same low heavy tone:

"She may not last out the day."

Inside of me I think to myself: "So much the better."

"Heavenly angels," my second philosophic voice sums up.

I go to your window and look out. "How beautiful

everything is," I say to myself as I sink into the peaceful green silence of the moment. You cough a short, impatient cough which brings me back to you and your room. I sit down again in the small armchair and smile at you.

"Sara," you whisper in almost no voice at all. "Hasn't she come yet?"

Her voice is loud or soft relative to the situation, my inner Mariana observes.

As if in reflection, I lower my voice to match yours.

"Sara cannot be here as often as she would like," I tell you in almost a maternal tone. "You know she now teaches in high school and classes have just started. That's why she can't afford to be absent. She did promise to come Friday afternoon and if it's all right with Andrés, she'll stay until Sunday. I'm hoping they can stay. Sara and I plan to go to town on Saturday. She says the church here is a wonderful example of antiquity, and I'd love to see it before I leave."

I tell you this so that you know that Friday and Sunday will be yours but Saturday is mine; we will however share it with you. Sara and I will be talking nonsense, laughing together, touching one another with our eyes, going back to the days when we were kids, when we wore braids and bows, petticoats with pulled-through ribbons. I love Sara, I confess to my other, my inner voice. To my amazement, the other Mariana does not respond. A warm silence embraces us both.

"How are you feeling?" I ask with sincere concern. You do not respond. You shrug your shoulders with displeasure so I can draw my own conclusions. "You are getting better," I venture. "You look better. If you go on eating the way you have, you will soon be well."

Then your voice: It surprises me with its artlessness.

"And you, what about all your ailments?"

"I'm all right." I succeed in forcing my voice to seem strong when I answer, so as not to reveal its deterioration.

"And the children? How are they?" you continue to question in a still feeble and defenseless little voice.

"Good! Still at it! Some are working, some studying, but thank God, they're all well," I say, more to reassure myself than you.

I think you have already talked enough about this so I change the drift of the conversation (I know it must be hard for you). I ask you the name of the tree which is completely covered with orange-red flowers. You seem to be smiling when you answer me. "People around here call it the 'wee-wee tree.'"

Now I understand why you smiled. Just as I am about to ask you if you heard it raining last night, I notice your eyes closing. "Go to sleep," I whisper to you. "Rest."

I leave the room with feelings of sadness and I don't know why.

Outside the rain has started again in a radiant sun burst. Berta's remark that "we're going to have some weather" materializes to my amazement as an incomprehensible storm..

I keep an eye on the downpour from the window of the room. It's a real macho downpour pounding away at the earth at its pleasure without rhyme or reason. Then the wind joins, shaking the unprotected branches powerfully and mercilessly, tearing off the leaves relentlessly, denuding the "morning brides" and daisies to demonstrate its power as Lord and Master of the universe.

At last the rain stops, as unexpectedly as it had come, and I hurry out to the balcony. The sun is shining again in full splendor and a fine silvery drizzle attempts to placate friend Earth with a quiet, peaceful rippling bath, allaying fears.

"Today we're up in the clouds," my more sober voice mocks as I harbor an assortment of crazy ideas which keep popping in and out of my frenzied brain.

"Do you see her? She's pregnant again." Agueda comments sardonically as she sits down at my side. I feel sympathy for her.

"And how is Mama Ernestina doing?" I ask to change the subject.

"She's sleeping," she answers almost indifferently.

She insists on pursuing the subject which obsesses

her. What a gossip she is!

"She's three months along," she says contorting her mouth in the direction of the little neighbor as she did before at the window of your room.

"That's not possible," I contradict her, "if she's just had a baby."

"Yes, but I was the one taking care of the other baby the night she gave birth. The women in that family are baby factories. They're worse than rabbits."

"I think you've made a mistake, Agueda," I reply somewhat aggravated. The day I came, I saw her nursing her baby boy."

"It's not a baby boy, it's a girl and just because she was nursing it don't mean nothing. It's to keep her boobs going. And she is pregnant. She has morning sickness. Believe me, it'll be the death of her."

It doesn't sound like anything Agueda would say, but Berta would! Yesterday she confided to me in her sing-song that when she got the morning sickness, you gave her a stern lecture and some purple garlic.

It is obvious that Agueda's speech is splashed with rich peasant verse utilized by Berta to embellish everything she says. Now I understand the ditty: "Women greedy for more and more... Gets belly she's not looking for." I smile at the double entendre and her healthy malice. Since Agueda's cruelty kills my desire to fantasize, I take advantage when she gets up to scare off Gringo who is chasing a hen and its chicks. I then set out for your room.

Seated at your side, I expect you to move, to open your eyes and look at me. You don't understand, do you? I rebuke you in my head. I want you to look at me, look at me, at me... at me...

It mortifies me that you do not move. In any case, I invite you to travel the pathways of life in silence. Not really to travel them. But for you and me together to pass through all the stations of my cross so that you understand where I'm coming from. Let me finger the black beads of my rosary, visit the dark corners and then light them up with a candle of *lignum vitae* (holy wood). Let's make it the day of our Candlemas! And burn everything! Make light, firelight to purify the flames, as the Martyrs did!

"But why?" asks the other Mariana, confused.

"I don't know why. Maybe to make her join in my deceptions, the only way she'll come to know me."

Over and above your silence and my mortification, I remember that Esteban and I are having dinner together tonight and that after we will talk, talk...and talk...

I didn't sleep much that night. I went to bed late because Esteban and I had so much to say to one another, in spite of Gringo who kept nagging and begging every minute. He is spoiled. He finally turned his back to me and leaped into Esteban's lap where he curled up comfortably like a child. Esteban rocked back and forth resting his hands on the dog's back, treating him like a child seeking solace on his Daddy's lap where he could peacefully fall asleep.

All of us are alone and lonely, I think to myself as I pull on my bathrobe, sadly confronting a naked truth. I should have asked about Emilia, but it's better this way. Sara will tell me. The thought of Sara coming on Friday fills me with joy. I shouldn't be thinking about it now. It's time to meet Esteban for breakfast.

I have a quick shower in your bathroom. It's the third day for me in your house and I haven't been invited by you. I dry myself with a towel that is not yours. That's how obstinate and insistent I am about not abusing your silence and your things; I do not touch anything you do not offer me. I examine how I look in my blue bathrobe. It is very becoming. I douse myself with perfume after I comb and arrange my hair with a certain air of coquetry. I put perfume on for him. Does that surprise you? For your son...my brother...that sounds better. I do it to obliterate the odor of your rancid flesh, the oily camphor-like smell of your withered skin, the odors of plants and poultices that inundate your room, your bed, your body. Forgive me. I know you can't help it. I really do love the fortress of your hard old bones and your constantly moving rough hands. I would like to retain the fragrance of a woman after a bath. Can you understand that I admire my brother as a man and love him as a brother? Who understands such things? In any case, it truly doesn't matter!

Esteban and I eat breakfast together as I had suggested and I have to say, mother dear, that one can't eat around here without being exposed to your smell. It's all over the place, stuck to every wall of your dreary, unprincipled house, enmeshed in cobwebs containing your traces and in every corner of your house...like distilled camphor, dense camphor—like vapors advancing furtively like smoke over the air, over whatever we eat, over our conversation, all of it dominating and dominated by you... you, Queen of worker ants, Queen Bee, Lady Bee, Big Bee, Giant Bee.

Since I do not want to be a nuisance, I take my pill after breakfast, make my bed, and go out-of-doors. I leave it to Berta to indulge you, scold you, and coddle you. You will naturally take out your ill-tempered morning mood on her.

The morning is clear and there is a stretch of tiny clouds unraveling in white tattered ribbons up in the indigo-blue sky...the air still bears the freshness of the night. It smells like Christmas...a Christmas of long ago, a sad one, lost in time in my memory.

"You were just a very little girl," Mariana murmurs pensively, her voice melancholic.

"Please! No!" I protest." Not today! Better keep your eye on that hen, the one with the grey spots. How merry she is! Scratching at the earth!"

"Looking for worms turned up by yesterday's rains."

The two of us smile, amused.

I hear Berta's footsteps and look in her direction. She is coming down the stairwell with a broom in her hand.

"Where is that damned cat?" she asks, out of breath and walking toward me.

Her face looks weary.

"What?" I question casually.

"That goddamn she-cat. If I didn't have to answer to God, I'd poison her. It beats me why your Mama loves her so much. The lousy beast is good for nothing, can't even catch mice. Look at that bitchy thing... mice all around her, and they nibble away at the sacks of corn, eat the grain and shit on the rice sacks...and there she sits, cool as a cucumber grinding out kittens...and that's all she's good for! She messes up everything. Everything in the kitchen has to be covered or put away. There's nothing she can't get her snout into. Just now she drank all the milk up I prepared for your Mama. And I fixed it with cinnamon and sugar. If I get my hands on her, I'll kill her."

The sun still fresh in the sky warms my back and a fragrant light breeze caresses us. Above our heads, hidden in the branches, a bird is spying on us, "bienteveo, bienteveo" (I see you, I see you), he is saying to advise us of his presence.

I sense that Berta's bad mood goes beyond the incident with Minina. I put my arms about her in a conciliatory gesture and ask: "What's wrong? You don't look well."

"It's because I can't sleep."

"Why?" I ask intrigued.

"Well, honey, it's that no-good family of mine. You should see the piles of dirty clothes! But I let them have it. Oh yes, I told them to wash their dirty bloomers in the creek. And

I told my husband to get the Hell out and work for a living. Seeing him in the house pisses me off. And I had two cups of black coffee without sugar. If I don't do something about them I'll end up like those scorpions that eat their own mother. They're not getting away with it! Not with me! They can go to Hell, see if I care!"

Mariana, she of whom I speak, makes a comment: "There you go! Women's Lib. It's finally come to this country!"

"And why shouldn't it?" I question angrily with such vigor that my voice leaps out of control. Fortunately Berta has already left. The smoke and smell of her cigarette trail behind her.

I see the flatlands from the top of the slope where your house stands. Before looking down beyond the bottom, I admire the variety and blend of greens; olive green, lime green, green mint, the green that turns yellow, the color of babies' "do-do" as my little princess of a grand-daughter would say. Everything perfectly balanced, discrete and harmonious, blending and complementing each other.

My eye rests on the roofs of the communal long houses where the chickens are clucking away, picking and eating, eating and picking. They eat fast to die fast. Why does it all have to end? Why does life have to end? This I ask myself. But I am not a philosopher. Whatever I am, I'm not that! Especially now when my only interest in life is to enjoy the sweet September morning air which gushes in from the just bathed, humid ravine. I breathe in deeply with pleasure. I immerse myself in its purity because I leave Sunday for home... for the city and pollution, to the noise of flies buzzing over a dead dog and the hum of my old electric fan blowing hot air over me and my forced silence.

Can I leave unhinged from you? It is a possibility. You no longer cause me that much pain. At a given moment between the night shadows and the first light of dawn, I hear you moaning. I rise and hasten to you in my bare feet. When I ask if something hurts, you purse the line of what is now almost a non-existent mouth and decline to answer. You persist in denying me. I persist too, in questioning you almost with kindly curiosity and you cause me no pain. I return to my bed and would you believe it? I fall asleep peacefully and resume dreaming a dream you have interrupted. "She is losing," my loyal Mariana whispers. She is almost dead to this world.

I sip the air on your balcony as I would coffee. The air from your yellow-green mountain is delicious! Just then, Berta calls me to breakfast. She already told me twice that you were sleeping. I hear her slippers click-clacking as she comes and goes.

One moment! I believe I hear something below! Of course... another rare bird from your mountain. Yes, that's it! I hear it clearly now. It is either singing, lamenting, or launching a macho lure, a courtship call, *á la* male-female: "chui, chui, chui." What is this crazy bird trying to say?

The baby of the child-mother has fallen asleep. The sun has wrought its wrath. All is violence beneath the white August sun. It appears that it has been forgotten that we are at September's end.

The little mother rocks away. And I yawn, my head nodding off. And again the "chui, chui, chui" of the macho bird. What are you plotting, wretched bird? Are you pecking away at her to gain possession of her? And after you do, will you love her in the same way? Love her forever? Forever? Liar! Liar! You will peck at her, deplume her, then leave her naked. Warm flesh for the macho bird to satisfy his hunger, his thirst, his delirium. However my fight is not with you today. Get thee hence, pecking bird and out of my sight! Today I go in search of peace, carpenter bird, borer of holes.

White! Blinding white! Dazzling sun! Rushes of hot air! Swells of air, heavy and thick moving back and forth. All at once, a light fresh breeze floats over me opening a thin, fine passage. I breathe deeply and the gentle wind makes me sleepy. I feel myself nodding off. Noises from your house make themselves apparent. The zinc roof, your roof is creaking, scandalized as it is by this white heat. A burning protest and I listen. I suspect I have a sense of foreboding that something strange is about to happen. I listen, then I hear:

"Mariana...Mariana...Mariana.."

Someone is calling me.

"Who is it? ...Who is calling me? Is it you, Mother? My mother..."

No, it isn't you.

It is a child's voice, a new one, a different one, a sparkling, crystal voice. I think back, search deep in my memory but can't locate it. It's romping about inside of me. Who is calling to me in this tiny tremulo?

"Mariana, Mariana, Mariana..."

A sudden feeling of depression! It's me! It's me! It's me! My voice is seeking me out. No, not mine, not my outer voice, nor my inner one, but one from my beginnings, a little thread of a voice summoning me anxiously. Beguiled, I walk towards it, pursuing it through a tunnel which is not light, light nor dark, dark, nor is it clear darkness. It is not cold and it is not hot. I smell nothing and see no color. No other sound is present except what may be coming from the child, the little child of my voice. There is scarcely a sound out of me and I am now in the light. And the voice, tremblingly soft and sweet, calls out to me. My small thread of a voice is now crying out, resounding through the room. I am choking, asphyxiated by the unfamiliar air. I long to go back to my little cave, to my small warm puffy pouch. Let the shell I dwell in orbit around! Let me move around in my amniotic well! It could be a lizard! A lizard! A lizard! Make the sign of the cross with your fingers, Marianita! Kiss the cross on your fingers, child! The evil eye. The laughter! The weeping! The fear! Run, Mariana, run! Here come the liana and the boogie man, the *guaraguo*! The owl is after you, child! The owl, Marianita! Owl! Owl! Owl!

The dogs barking and Berta's footsteps awaken me. I am still on your balcony. The flies zoom and buzz over me, sniffing at me and marveling. Here and in the tunnel where there is no light or dark I continue to trace the thread of my voice.

Berta, still intent on listening to the "cui, cui, cui" from the *caoba* tree, scolds:

"Hey, you already screwed the little gal, you low life."

"What are you talking about?"

"The bird. Can't you hear him chuckling?"

I get up and follow her into the kitchen to eat lunch and I savor her every word: "I made some delicious yellow corn tortillas and a cup of freshly-strained coffee." What more could I ask for?

Today I propose to serve you your lunch.

"You must mash the rice," this, almost like an order from Berta before she leaves.

Obediently I mash the rice, with your spoon, almost to a grind, but I do not serve it to you. I give you only the thick rich liquid. I don't want a repeat of what you did with the codfish yesterday.

"Codfish...a little piece of codfish," you insisted in a whine. I do understand. I also have a yen for something salty at times. But, what did you do? You sucked on it all afternoon and all night and then began to push it out through the long, fine corners of your mouth, piece by piece string by string of dry, white codfish. I collected all the shreds in my handkerchief patiently, in the hope I would see one of your little smiles again. When I entered your room and you heard my footsteps, you opened your eyes, squinting; you called to me in a soft whisper meant only for you and me. It was then that I lost the battle. I confess I can never give up on you. I cannot reject you.

I know I am ambivalent about our problems, our lives, but even if you hurt me and I hurt you, I do love you. Yes, I do. I have loved you every hour of our lives, in spite of the fact that you were not there for me...in spite of the bitterness and resentment which kept growing within me like a venomous weed, enraging us and eating away at all of us...implacable enemies. I'm telling you this because it's better that you know it. "Like a chicken without a head," Berta says when she refers to her husband "Cajlito."

I'm sick of the whole damn business. I repeat, the same old business; I make myself bitter with it. That's why I insist on knowing what I represented for you back then, in the age of confusion. Roots? A transplanted bulb? Uprooted from my yellow-green country-side, from my rose apple fragrance and my sparrow nests, from the fine, clear mornings of silver mist and orange hued dusks?

So many things are lost. No more reciting of the grey-bead rosary, no quivering candles, no shades of orange at nightfall. Nothing left of everything that I loved, because I also lost you.

Rest easy! I don't mean to sound bitter. I do understand why you had to leave me. Simply put, the moment had arrived for you to change your life and I was in the way. You probably were aware of the difficulties a single woman would have with a small child. Not an easy thing!

And it wasn't easy for you to separate yourself from your other children.

It wasn't easy for them, either, especially Esteban. How old was he when you and I went to live in the country, when you separated from Papa? Eight years old? I ask because Esteban remembers so many little things around that time, Mama.

I remember one incident especially. One afternoon we were playing in the house. It was raining hard and Obdulia would not let us go outside. We were lying stretched out on the floor. But not Sara. She was seated, her back against the wall, knitting. At that time she was being taught to knit in school and would hang on to that needle and thread for dear life.

I don't know how the conversation started, but he said: "When you and Mama left, Uncle Lorenzo came to pick up your things; they carried you out because you couldn't walk. You couldn't do anything because you were such a cry-baby. You were an awful cry-baby." He said just that.

Sara stuck up for me. "Don't pay any attention to him," she said as she continued knitting. "He's a jealous cat and he's bad. Want to know what he did? He caught a couple of little lizards, put them in empty bottles and stoppered them up." It was true. He had done it. He deprived them of air to make them die.

I didn't know then how to interpret what he had said about me and I finally tossed it off as a joke. Now, I think that things like that stayed with him. Furthermore both he and Sara resented my being in the house when I came back. It took a long time for us to be a real family.

But Papa has to share the blame too. You know how he used to sit down in his chair after supper to read his newspaper. He would sometimes call me when he was through and say: "Come here by me, Marianita, sit with me." On his knees! And I was a big girl! with such long legs that when he rocked, my feet almost grazed the floor with my shoes. I had long hair and he liked to pass his calloused hand over my head; I didn't like it because my hair would get messed and I had to keep cutting knots and loose ends. But I always kept quiet. He was expressing his understanding in this way. He was aware that I needed a bit more tenderness and attention at that time than did Sara or Esteban. Papa was very good.

It doesn't mean you weren't. And it doesn't mean you are being censured indirectly by what I say. No, Mama. Not directly or indirectly. I'm not the one to pass judgment on you. Just being your daughter doesn't give me the right. On the contrary, when I grew up and learned more about life, I had nothing but admiration for your willpower and your courage to have broken with everything. I admire you now.

What I fail to understand is why you allowed Papa to carry you off to live in your mother-in-law's house. O.K. It is true. She was alone, she was a widow and he felt this responsibility. He could have resolved the situation otherwise, for example, by living close by, but not together, not in contention, just close by.

It was the same when you shut yourself away in the country. Mama, I did adore the country. You know that. I adored Grandma María. I was happy with her and my fondest memories are still memories of her despite all that has happened.

But I can't help asking: What did you gain by being there? What did you hope to accomplish? Surely you were consumed by such an uneventful existence without challenge or advantage. Having lived in the city in the first years of marriage must have developed a taste in you for other things. Living in a city is quite different, The habits we form, once established, are almost impossible to break.

Tell me about it! I was the one who took forever to get accustomed to my new life. That was bad enough but it was worse because I had to stay with Papa in his house forever, not just for summer vacation.

Why did I insist on remembering these things? As if time had passed only in vain? You certainly look at it as senseless. I agree; it doesn't make sense! But my other voice, the one inside of me, tells me to share it all with you, to relive the past. It tells me that reliving the past is good for the soul, not for the purpose of finding fault but for forgiveness and understanding.

Come along with me, Mother Ernestina. Let's walk together. I'll take you along the paths of my memory.... See? I'm wearing my white dress to attend Mass, the dress you made for me to celebrate my first communion in the San Bonifacio Chapel. The organdy, thin crystal-like cloth with lace edging. It had three ruffles and a white belt at the waist. Let's walk. You carry the bag and I'll take Milton the dog. Where did you sleep that night, that first night? I stayed in Papa's house. My brothers and sisters were there and I was definitely there too. But you? Let me guess. Let me guess. You went with your friend Haydee, right? The one who married the Peruvian sailor and later went out of her mind.

The moment you left I felt the house didn't like me. I spent all night looking for your scent in Sara's bed ... in her long hair. I searched everywhere, in the covers, the mosquito netting, the pillow. Wakeful and anxious, I listened to the nocturnal sounds of the city, noises familiar to me but at the same time strangely new and terrifying...pigeon feet gliding over the zinc roof, tiny *jarriero* feet over the wood ceiling, the creaking of the house and the intermittent howls of the dog. Your dog, who had taken to hiding under the house from the moment you left. When you were in the living room chatting with my step-mother, he set about to explore the house, but when your scent was gone, what can I say? ...the two of us wept. Poor little pup with his yellow spots and sad drooping ears. He cried for you! You didn't come to fetch him and he cried; he finally gave up and died. Since then I'm no longer fond of dogs.

I sing to myself softly and look out of your "patey" as Berta refers to the patio of your house. I am humming. You don't know it—I never told you—but I never forgave him for abandoning me, too. The two of you took off. You and he.

That naughty little bleary-eyed short-haired mutt with his droopy tail. As if there were no one left to hold it up for. But that wasn't all.

Do you remember Marilu, Sara's doll? Marilu was made of white porcelain. No, she wasn't exactly white. She was small with a pot belly and had a little round face, chubby cheeks with rose splotches. Do you remember? And her little mouth was painted crimson red. The Three Wise Men brought her to Sara. At your house on Retiro Street, where for a short time you sold trinkets. It's as if I see it now and realize all the water that has flowed under the bridge since then.

Those were the days when you adored Sara. And I swear to you that I understood, I really did...with her green eyes and those lashes she had, like a Sevres doll (a collection of the finest dolls). Why not? Why shouldn't you have been crazy about her? And you weren't the only one! Sara always had the gift of drawing people to her; she was so sweet and friendly! Of course, she had lots of friends. But not me! I had only a few, but I never envied her, not for that reason at least. But the doll. I cried myself sick over that doll for a long time; it seemed like centuries. The Three Wise Men never left a doll like that for me in your house. At first I cried out loud for everyone to see, to find out whether I could elicit sympathy and understanding, but no one paid any attention to me. Later I resigned myself and cried in a corner. All alone in the corner with my sobs and the spiders. I wailed as I never had, just like when I scraped my knees on the iron fence Papa put up when the prostitutes moved in next door and when I was punished for not scrubbing the pots.

Now I understand why I cried so. I couldn't find words to articulate the real reason for my unhappy state. I thought it was because I did not have a doll just like Sara's. But no,

Mama. It wasn't the doll; it was the favoritism you displayed toward my sister. God! I still choke up! What would it have cost to have bought two dolls alike? Sorry! Don't pay any attention to me! I'm not accusing you of anything at this stage in the game. You did give me a present which you probably thought was more appropriate, But what did you expect? I was consumed with jealousy. I was totally obsessed! Then guess what happened? The poor doll died!

Afterward, Sara made the cutest dresses with the help of Zoila Borrero, our neighbor, the one who lived across the street, two houses down from us. Do you remember her? You must have known her. When you and Papa got married her family was already living there. They were the oldest residents on Baldorioty Street. Once I overheard something Grandma told Obdulia. She said that when she and Grandpa Serafin were thinking of buying a house, it was Montserrate Borrero who advised them that there was one for sale almost next-door to the one he planned to buy.

He bought the house and Zoila was born and raised there. Later she married that fat man who owned the hardware store next to the Bonbonera. His name was...let me think...I remember now. His name was Ramón Esteves. *Don* Moncho was what everyone called him. They married and lived across the street. In time Zoila's parents died and the couple moved into their house, her inheritance.

The poor woman! It was rumored that she had consumption; they used to say she looked like a dried-out herring. I can't say if it was so. I can only say that she was a lively, happy person despite her appearance and that she was very skinny. She was so pale, you could see the veins through her transparent skin, despite the powder and rouge she always used.

So, Sara and she sewed clothing for the doll; the nicest dresses you can imagine! Some for after the morning bath and some for after the evening bath when she dusted her with yellow powder which smelled of dried flowers supplied by cockroach Martina de Zoila. But one Saturday afternoon about two o'clock, the poor little dolly died. The wood floor had not dried yet...

I think about those days and can see Obdulia, a yellow kerchief on her head, and her nose shining with sweat. She is kneeling...scrubbing away. She is scrubbing, scrubbing for you with lots of soap and ammonia. Sara and I fetch the water. Buckets and buckets of water to remove dirt from the previous week and to be ready for next week's dirt. The house is full of cooking odors...chicken, sweet basil, mugwart, and patchouli roots...for good luck, of course...spells and charms: lemon tarts, sword protector of house and king. How did you and Papa fall in love? I have asked myself this question so many times. But I'm not bringing it up now. "Not now or ever," my shadow voice counsels, a bit preoccupied.

Her constant interjections annoy me and I let it be known. There are times when I must cut her short. "Oh excuse me," it says in a sarcastic tone which seems to be mocking. A copy of my own voice. Most exasperating and she thinks it is funny. She has the habit of mimicking me like a naughty little monkey, even using my intonation. She is irritating me now. Therefore there are times when I speak in monosyllables like: Yes, no, you, me, just because of it. She does hide sometimes. Isn't it the height of absurdity that I spend my time in constant struggle with people I can't even see?

My! We were talking about the house when I shifted direction. On Saturdays, sometimes white daffodil plants were brought up to your corner in the sitting room to be returned to the patio on Monday to your place under the witch's broomstick, where, according to Obdulia those twisted creatures sleep like she-cats after their nightly rounds. There were the Saturdays smelling of oil rags polishing the furniture in grandmother's sitting room. Remember Grandma's furniture? Your mother inherited it and adored it. In time I came to love it, too. I can still see the sofa with its two places, and the arm chair along with the other chairs, all oval backs and wicker seats. Papa painted, glued and mended them every year before Christmas. They were molded to our bodies. Then on Saturdays there were the doilies in a pineapple stitch, adorning the lamp tables, the marquisette curtains and your portrait. Why was that portrait always there for all to see? It was no longer appropriate for it to occupy such a preferential place. I guess it was grandmother's idea. After all, it was her house and she probably left it there to remind poor Obdulia (she never did get along with her) that you were her son's first wife and the mother of her grand-children. How incredibly cruel!! You and Papa looking out at all of us from that wedding picture. My father, very handsome in his white linen suit, his cane and watch chain...and that look in his eye! "I take this woman for better or worse; I will care for her, love and protect..." I always wanted to have his eyes. They were small and brown and shaded by long lashes, like my sister's... which reminds me. We were talking about the doll. I was telling you that the poor thing died... What I didn't say is how it happened. Esteban killed it. He put a stone in his rubber sling-shot, aimed it at Marilu's head and broke it to pieces. Just like that! I was convinced he did it for me. In time I was disillusioned because one day when he was older, he confessed he had gotten tired of my whining and complaining. "I got sick of it!" he told me. Now you know! He lost patience with me that day and poor little Marilu was stoned to death! Then it was Sara's turn to cry. If only you had been there... but you weren't... You had already left the city. You had either sold your business or gone bankrupt or maybe it wasn't yours and you only ran it. I have no idea and do not remember details. But you certainly weren't there! All I remember is that the next year shortly before the annual visit of The Three Wise Men, I lived obsessed with your return. Only God knows! "Dear Lord, make her come...even if it's only for this one time!" I would say this prayer every night before going to bed. I thought that one time would suffice to give warning to the Three Forgetful Wise Men that in houses where there are two little girls, they must leave two dolls. Each one of the little girls should have the chance to love it, fondle it and tell it stories... spoil it also as they wished to be spoiled by having it... even if the two little girls are not quite alike... even if one is rosy and pretty and plump and the other straight and skinny as a stick like the doll I finally wound up with, the one whose arms refused to fold over her raggy chest and whose eyes were always in a fixed stare; she had a bleary look under her eyelashes. I know you would never have tortured yourself with such nonsense. I said it before. I was a silly little simpleton.

"You had a good sleep," I say to you when you open your eyes. You blink and look searchingly around the room. You smile at me when you recognize the familiar surroundings.

"How are you?" you ask me.

It should have been I to ask.

"How are the children?" you ask again.

I had already informed you that they were well, but it doesn't matter. I repeat the answer and we smile at one another. I continue:

"Do you know that the doctor thinks you are much better?"

"Were you here?" you ask gravely.

"Yes, not only does he find you better, but he thinks if you are up to it, you will soon be able to get out of bed... But you must be careful...just from the bed to the chair and the chair to the bed for a while, and no funny business."

My concern pleases you. I can see you brighten up.

"I just don't want you to be sick and dizzy again," I persist in order to add to your satisfaction.

I note you looking over at the little Virgin standing upright in the roughly hewn house. I say it is a bit warm and that I will be leaving. I imagine you have a good deal to say to the Virgin, just as I have to you. So let it just be between the two of you.

I sit down at the other end of the porch where shadows have already fallen. I give thanks to God. Agueda is busy attending to your laundry; I know that as soon as she is through, she will come out and sit with me. I'm exhausted and I pretend to be asleep to avoid hearing more of her stories. I do it not only because of that, but because I want to think about you.

I told you how I felt uprooted so I could reproach you, but it wasn't right. You had no way of knowing and it is really not true. I don't feel that way, at least not now. Yes, I used to when life was a living Hell for me. A lot of self-criticism and demands on myself for a full account of what I did...day after day...night after night...about what I had done, what I didn't do or what I should have done. God! What an idiotic waste of energy! What relentless pursuit! What a thing I had about putting myself down! Torturing myself with every kind of nonsense! It was chaos! Utter chaos!

But not now! No more! By working, I have picked myself up by the bootstraps. Little by little I have become the Mariana that I used to be. I am still not doing the knitting or the lace and needle-work, but at least I am reading and occasionally writing notes, trying to see whether I can be cured of this leprosy. It's one of the reasons I have come here. The new me must cleanse herself of the refuse of which you

are part (forgive me for saying this) but it was a biological
accident that brought me into this world. I say accident
because I think I entered your life inopportunely and late, at
a time when you were no longer looking for additions. I
understand! It was the wrong time!

What is sad is that it took me so long to break bonds
which, if I may be permitted to say, distorted my life, ruined
my health and made me what I am. Stop play-acting! Open
your eyes and look at me! Look at this old body, more than a
half-century in years, with a face ready to fall in and wrinkled
over hollowed out skin, deformed hands... all produced by my
sickness. A sickness which indeed has been faithful to me.
I'm not saying this to arouse your pity. You know how much
I detest pity! I tell you this so that when you complain to me,
that you acknowledge that all of us have a cross to bear.

I feel good inside when I can talk openly to you. The
problem is I frequently forget it. I am so devastated when I
come back, even momentarily, I am bitter with self-pity. But
one day I will divest myself of this entirely, as your ex-
mother-in-law would say, the grandmother who tried to
replace the beautiful Marilu with an old rag doll, a remnant of
the family, one without a soul...until she learned to love me.
So much so that later there was no other so dear. Where can
Lucía be? If I knew, I would still be sleeping with her.

Yes, I said there was something left of me inside. It's
true. Something which perhaps you cannot see, although you
may look at me anxiously wanting to see me without my
shadows or child-like pretexts. There is a renewed desire for
me to do things, emerge again. I am a fountain but you must
be aware that I am emerging from a well.

There is nothing left of Arturo's and my home, unless
you want to attach some importance to the walls, the doors,

the windows, the pictures...and the rooms with empty beds. I sleep in mine, Arturo, no longer in his. He is gone, forever. He has gone in search of what he believes life owes him. There was nothing left to do but give him a divorce. If you had known, you wouldn't have approved. But the situation was intolerable. We became very polite to one another and very sparing in our conversation. The root of the problem probably was that he woke up one day, took a look at himself in the mirror and decided that life had passed him by. A life squandered on me and the children and the responsibilities of marriage. On that day, he examined his graying hair, probed his wrinkles and came to the conclusion he hadn't much time left. He was terrified! And I, the other unhappy creature, was there, not knowing what to do in a situation which arrived without warning. In the meantime, he took to rolling in the hay with all sorts of women and robbing the cradle, too. My world came tumbling down. I received phone calls, I found notes and letters, even a photograph from some little fool, a photo from her graduation. A young girl, the same age as María Esperanza! You would have burned it without a second thought! I put it up on the refrigerator with a magnetic clip; that's what was left of my dignity! To let him know that I knew! "The most absurd of absurdities," you would have said and rightly so.

There were days when I would wake up serene, purposely serene. I concentrated on it. I counseled prudence to him. Be careful of the people with whom you associate; don't expose yourself to diseases they are talking about so much today. But on other days, I became a devil, the Devil himself. What can I say? Something turned and twisted inside of me. I couldn't understand this search of his, the deception, the illusion, the desire to touch heaven with his hand. No. I

was too old too. I am old! So what? There's no going back! I
wasn't frightened or troubled by it; I didn't deceive myself
with false pretensions of youth. But he...well, the truth is
Mama...I didn't understand. I didn't know what to do. Sometimes I played the role of the resigned martyr and other times
I was the Devil incarnate. The jealousy, the rage, the humiliation blasted out of my mouth in gushes...cruel words, corro-
sive ones...and the castrating postures, descending to his level
out of sheer spite. The scenes we had! The violent, painful and
bitter scenes! They left me drained and exhausted. Then there
was the terror that one night he would not return home, that
he would stay out there. Yes, his only refuge was in flight.
Then, the fear of not hearing the key in the lock, not hearing
him rummaging for food in the refrigerator, not hearing
noises from the bathroom. He might be leaving me! Imagine!
He might not return! A bitterly untenable situation, a desper-
ate one. But a constant. We did have a respite. Arturo came
around little by little. I suppose he had had it. At least I thought
so because he appeared to be resuming his normal routine. He
was not exactly his old self. If only you had seen him! I could
have killed him! He went around with a pathetic smile on his
face, a smoke screen for hypocritical martyrdom! It dawned
on me that he looked upon me as an obligation...a burden he
could not renounce. He saw me as a mother...he told me this.
He began to complain of back pains, of this and that, and
without discussing it, he moved out of our room and slept in
another. One night, after Esperanza went off to the university
(she was the last to leave home), he came back to sleep in my
bed, but he was somehow changed. I believe it was on a
Tuesday that I was told he had another woman.

　　　　When he left my bed, I accepted it wordlessly. I didn't
feel resigned. After all, I've no vocation for the holy sister-

hood nor for sainthood. But the matter of another woman was something else again. Now it was not one of those one-night floozies he insisted on flitting around with, his eyes glazed and greedy. No, this was a good, decent woman, well educated and, of course, much younger than I. Her name was...and this will make you laugh...I did... her name was Fabiana. A friend I met one afternoon in the drug store told me. She couldn't let me go without filling me in on the news. My sympathies are with him. That name always reverberating in his mouth would keep him reminded of me. Later, I assumed he didn't ask for a divorce out of compassion for me and you know my weakness. I can accept anything but pity. I can't take it. I felt cast off, humiliated, obviously. So, one October morning, I let him go. Without a second thought, I opened the door to his cage, and he flew away hypocritically joyful and with resignation, free at last from the boredom that consumed him in our home, my home for the personal effects.

Afterward there was my struggle with the lonely house, which stubbornly did not allow me to forget. The emptiness when he left! How can I explain it so that you could understand? It was the absence of everything he was...the foam drippings of his shaving cream, the drool his toothpaste left in the sink, his dirty clothing which he left everywhere, which used to drive me wild. Things that elicited so many reproaches from me. And would you believe what happened then? Believe it or not, I longed for him, for all of it!

You would have reacted otherwise. You would never have done what I did. You always were in control. You were the creator of your destiny and the destinies of those around you. But I am not like you. You always dominated. I do not say this in a pejorative sense. You smile when I say this. I say it with respect and admiration of your strength and your control under certain conditions. I am more like the song which goes:

> If you leave, be happy, be gay
> Forget what I was, what I used to say
> And I standing here in my window
> Will see the morning tinged with grey.

As for me, I was always tinged with grey: morning, noon and night...even in my dreams. And what about the insomnia that troubled me? and the sleeping pills, the aspirin, the constant headaches? God! Those headaches! The state they would leave me in! There were days I walked around in a daze and I spent them wandering around the house in my bathrobe. Just as I said, like a Zombie, nothing more, nothing less...the "*loca*" of the house. I scared myself when I looked in the mirror. I almost died, Mama. I dried out and became skin and bone.

Just imagine the house! After nineteen years, for the first time without the smell of that man! Without the smell of his body, his after-shave lotion, his cigarette smoke. Without his footsteps, his voice, his presence which never seemed to have occupied much space, but how he filled everything. Searching for him in this way, searching for his odors...I laugh about it now. It reminds me of the daughters of Bernarda Alba who yearned for the smell of a man in a house without men.

I laugh about it now, but not in those days. Bones ached that I never knew I possessed. I discovered wrinkle upon wrinkle. It was then I realized how grey I had become. I had grey hair. I tint it now just as he does. I think I turned grey overnight. It was when he was insisting on making up for lost time. I was almost delirious with pain penetrating my insides because there was no avenue of escape for them. It's your pain alone and cannot be shared. No matter how much sympathy people may feel, it's barely an awareness. It's very common in this country for a man to have more than one woman. Two, three or four, in fact, to give him his true pleasures. Like roosters in a hen house, animals, studs, whose main job it is to lay the females and beget children...with this pathetic excuse..."You bear my name; you're the lady of the house and I provide the food and all that you may require..." So what? What value does this have for a woman who has become old at her man's side? Tolerating him, bearing him like a cross? Wife, lover, nurse, servant, secretary, all in one. In the end, to whom do you matter? You end up destroyed, torn apart, and writhing in your own pain, which is yours alone. You try to rise above it, pull yourself together because you are destroying yourself with bitterness, and you can't...it doesn't happen. You panic and look for strength in the one thing left to you...your faith. You pray, light candles, kneel in supplication, all in vain. It doesn't come...it simply doesn't happen. You torture yourself masochistically and perversely. Why weren't you a better daughter, a better mother, a better wife? You torture yourself about everything. Then you want to know why and who tired of whom first? Who got fed up first? A good question! Now indeed you are converted into your own worst enemy, incarnate! There is always the accusing finger. It was your fault, Mariana. Shutting yourself off, your silences. You didn't listen, didn't submit! Submit? I didn't yield? Didn't acquiesce? Why should I have? Why? Maybe I don't have rights? What about my dreams, my ambitions, my desires? My soul was agonizing and he was asking me to listen to him, to understand him and his needs. And me? Who was giving me understanding? Me? Who was listening to me?

I shall never forgive him. This need he had to live it up

was probably stirring in him for a long time. It wasn't until he started comparing his old broken down wreck of a woman beside him in bed, with other beautiful young, happy, lively ones, that he calculated it was time to exchange me for one of them. I understand. I recognize that we all have the right to choose...to live our own lives as we please. But I will never forgive him for hurting me so much, so terribly.

It's because of him that I've developed the habit of looking inward, because of him that the voice of my silence inadvertently came to life; the voice of my subconscious, if you wish to call it that. I learned to dialogue with it, to speak of things with someone who existed only for me. I call her Mariana. It is the voice of my twin, the other me, and she has a right to the name. Although I should call her Solitude since she was born from it, of solitude. I'm surprised that she has not once interrupted our conversation.

"She had nothing to say," she murmurs suddenly."You have said it all."

"Everything?" I inquire, amazed.

"Almost everything."

It seems to me that she is smiling when she adds: "You can save the rest for tomorrow, right?"

Today the sun refuses to come out. And I was the one who rose early to watch for that very pampered entity and it frustrated me. I compensate for my disillusion by breathing the magical air of dawn. It is time for daybreak and the air is fresh. I sip it in. Careful! Too many mouthsful and you're intoxicated! It is so pure, it goes to your head. Everything is moist, bathed in dew. Drops of water, like small diamonds, slide noiselessly over the leaves. a humming bird buries his long beak into the heart of the island, as he flaps his little paper-like wings at giddying speed. "It is a humming bird," whispers Mariana softly, not to scare him off.

Wait! Even though the sun has still not displayed its colors, it can't hide its light. Now bit by bit, light creeps out, like a roguish cat, still and discrete. It emerges stealthily behind a heavy cloud. It diffuses in silence, opening up like a rose. There is no hurry. One moment all is grey, then yellow-grey, then yellow over brown. It disperses, diffuses. The battle is won. Blues and oranges blend. It's done. Day is alight!

"Good morning, Mama," I greet you affectionately.

I raise the mosquito netting to listen for your answer which is not forthcoming. However, you open your eyes. You stare at me. Curiously enough, I believe you are studying me.

"It was really cold last night, wasn't it?" I persist, using the same tender tone. "I had to wear Esteban's socks to keep my feet warm. I couldn't fall asleep, my ankles hurt so much. But I was here twice to check on you. I worried that you might have uncovered yourself or that you wanted something. But you were fine...fast asleep. It was the first time I saw you sleeping so soundly without sedatives. Good! There is nothing better than natural sleep! Do you want me to remove the mosquito netting? I can open the window too, to warm up the room. These are the months of the year when it is so humid."

You smile.

My mind is racing like the wind. What are you thinking about? I hang the rolled-up mosquito netting to the nail on the wall. Then I open the window just a little. I think how awful it would be if she were to catch cold. She must be tired, tired of staying in bed. I turn to you with a cheerful look:

"Do you know what day it is today? It's Friday, Mama. Something special this afternoon. Let's see. Who is coming here to visit you today? Try to remember. You know."

You play along shyly:

"Today...? Sara. She is coming after four if there's no teachers' meeting."

"There is no meeting this afternoon, Mama," I say, to quiet her fears." Even if there were, I assure you, she would not go. She promised to come early and she'll be here."

I note that you have spoken a good deal more than usual and that it cost you some effort. I feel uneasy and continue to cover up my concern:

"Did Berta tell you that her oldest daughter will be here today? No? Well, she really didn't say anything to me either. I suppose she will help with the cleaning."

I sit down in the armchair thinking this will be a bad day for my bones. I will have to take two pills instead of the one and do a bit of walking. It always works. I turn this thought off and substitute another.

"Would it annoy you if I cut roses for the vases?" I ask, expressing a desire I've had since yesterday. "The roses with the hundreds of petals which are shedding. I have never seen so many buds. Perhaps it's the manure Berta sprinkles around the bushes. Shall I cut some daisies too? I can put them over there on the dressing table. You always loved daisies."

"And jasmines," you whisper with a sigh.

"Yes, Mama," I say, "I know. But the jasmine is a May flower and we are still in September. But who knows, with all the rain we've been having, they might bloom before their time. Remember the song I was singing to you yesterday? I wrote it the day Paloma parked herself in the kitchen. I wish you could see her. She is the most beautiful collarina I've seen in my life. I wrote the song the day she arrived. It's not that it's so special but that only you, Paloma, and I have heard it. I sing it when the children are gone and when I feel terrible emptiness. Yesterday I tried to sing it to you. This time I'm doing it for another reason:

> Night was falling
> You were drowsing. I was singing
> "I am a dove dying of love
> I am a dove living in shadow
> No longer eager to see the sun..."

You enter and leave my silly song. I insist that you hear it even half-way through. My little song drapes over you, wrapping itself around you like mist over a mountain peak. "Nananananina nananananina..."

I sing an old song to you about an ancient tree dying of solitude and abandonment. Then back to the dove, back to the old tree, my voice rocking over you in a simple song, cradling you and releasing the anguish of the bitterness which has eaten at me for years, through the gentle melody. It is at this moment that I discover that it is easier to sing to you than to forgive you. Though both seem to be the same thing, the word forgiveness, as demanding and relentless as it is, becomes difficult, and it cost me plenty to say it to you, but there it is. So I said it to you in a song, fluttering over you, exhausted and melancholy...the roles reversed...with you, my small child and I...your little mother. My poor little bad girl, with the burned out strands of grey hair and little bony face, smooth and stretched, ironed out. You always had lovely skin. It had a toned-down shine which I always admired. It was so lovely; and your wonderful, long hands, the hands of a queen clasping the rails of your bed. They look almost as though they were asleep. I stare at your hands and grant forgiveness in my trembling woeful song...for all they could have done for me, I forgive them. For all they didn't do, I forgive them...this, as

I twist and twist again and again in the armchair. Then I pass in front of your window and meet the light of dusk, almost night, a timorous bride before surrender. I walk over to the dressing table where the little Virgin stands overcome by sleep as you are, waiting for her veil to be fastened. I search out her gaze which I find passing over us, over you and over me. Not resting over us, passing over us. Even so, I feel she loves us as we love one another. I approach your bed. I speak quietly to you through the mosquito netting: "Tomorrow is Friday, Mama. Sara will be here and we might not get much chance to talk to one another." I had already told you I would be leaving on Sunday because of my doctor's appointment on Monday; I can't cancel it. I then kiss you on the forehead and promise I will return. Then I go to bed. I leave you in good company...

Sunday! Yesterday's day was so short! I hope we didn't disturb you! Sara and I had so much laughing to catch up on! And we didn't exclude you! The two of us laughed about you and with you. I saw you smiling at our nonsense. That's why I worked up the enthusiasm to invite you to come with me—on an imaginary trip—to come home with me.

Esteban and I are now leaving in the old jeep. I admire his skill in moving it from one spot to another to avoid pot holes—which we jokingly call craters. I am glad you are not physically present. You would be driven mad by the crazy exploits of your son. You've no idea how much I enjoy these trips! I like traveling the old roads which connect the small towns of the interior of the island.

We descend bumping along, jumping over craters, our hearts in our mouths—tumtumtumtum—scared out of our wits. To allay my fears, I watch the road. We go down snaking along the edge of ravines which at times are incredibly deep, almost always abysses above the river which attracts our attention from down below, a noisy, tumultuous sound because of the abundance of water it has swallowed. It is the hurricane season; there is no holding back the rains during the rest of the year. Therefore it moves downward swollen and puffed up, like a turkey, kicking about like a drunkard and munching on things no one knows anything about.

Esteban and I talk. At first he responds in monosyllables; he is poised for any surprise he might meet on the road. I am the one who leads him into the yesterdays of our todays without his realizing it. For the moment our present is relegated to second place. We dust off memories. I harass him with mine. He agrees or disagrees with me in a half-smile and adds details unknown to me, memories of his which have nothing to do with me. He is very intelligent and I listen to him, fascinated.

The two of us are running down the lane of the village house of our yesterday. It is quite dark. Of course, we are traveling in the small Ford he is driving. It is a broom stick with a sardine can stuck up the middle. A rather rusty nail is jammed through a narrow hole in the tin. Fastened to the nail is a strip which in better days might have been used to force the rusty nail to move up and down because the tin is bent. A farce of an automobile horn! The Ford horn! Aguu...aguu...and the driver...grun...grun..., starting up the powerful motor. I never did discover how he managed to keep the headlights, the lamp of the little Ford, from falling off the sardine can. The poor, dizzy, blinking little things acted out a death wish. Its faint yellow light danced about: "Now I'm on, now I'm not."

Suddenly, a warning from the driver: "Hang on!!" He's about to do something fast! Take a dangerous turn or stop suddenly...All of us are prepared. I grab him tightly around the waist. Argelia, my friend and neighbor, holds on to mine...to be prepared for the unexpected. All at once, a truck! The little Ford turns violently, the lane twists and we land up on the side of it. Laughing with tears in our eyes, we fall on top of a terrified cat making his get-away. He and I relive the incident.

"Remember the carnival? the teacher with the big rear-end, the coconut candy they used to make at home?" I choke with laughter. "Remember Obdulia's face when she counted the candies we were supposed to sell, counting over and over again. The count never came out..."

"How could it come out straight when you ate practically all of them?" he says, laughing with pleasure.

"It wasn't me! It was Pipa who did it." I say in self-defense when I can control my laughter.

He becomes serious and says:

"Did you know that the ants ate Pipa up...?"

"No, I didn't," I say pretending surprise so that he'll tell me.

I actually do know. I often saw queen ants load their cargo piece by piece burying it in their small caves beneath the floor, black with urine and dirt in the house where Pipa Carraro nursed her diabetes with coconut candy and sesame balls.

There are so many things to remember! The tobacco growers...the women workers...Meeting of the Free Federation of Workers, meetings at which Esperanza always appeared. She was a co-founder. And I never missed one. I had to come. Always up front, half-asleep and bored to death!

"Do you remember the speaker from San Juan? the one with the handle-bar mustache? and the fat guy with the short legs who always wore long-sleeved shirts? He was always sweating."

"Those guys were all Communists," Esteban hastens to add with assurance.

"Weren't they Socialists?"

"What are you talking about, girl? They were Communists. Do you know who the leader was...that old guy! the Spaniard! The one with the suspenders. They were saying that Nadal..."

He smiles obliquely in denial, wagging his finger from right to left.

"No! Not him! It was the Spaniard. Do you know who told me? Emilia Josefa. She was chummy with all of them. They used to go to her house after the meetings..."

What intrigue!

He says nothing else. Memories are flooding his head. I always believed he had become a man there, with Esmeralda, the prostitute, who was like an Indian princess. His silence has just given credence to it. Even so, I ask: "What ever happened to that beautiful woman...the tall, dark one...?"

"Esmeralda? She poisoned herself with Lysol! They say it was because of a Spanish sailor..."

The subject ended with this. Nevertheless I felt drawn to the memory of Esmeralda and the "pigeon house." I can't put those memories aside either.

It was my passion to look for an opening in the iron fence where I could peek, to dream of being one of those elegant, beautiful women, so fragrant with heliotrope perfume. God! What an ambition! Aspirations of being a whore! I laugh so heartily that Esteban turns to look at me. I tell him that Argelia used to say that when she grew up, she would go to live in that house. I do not tell him that it wasn't the eyes of the eleven year old Argelia that bulged with passion, jet black eyes, but mine with their angry envious luster when I glared at Papa for having built the fence grating to separate our house from the one of vice and perdition.

The blue mountains and the fresh earth remained behind during our conversation. The city dressed in its Sunday best with its smells and noises comes forward to greet us "Agua-ca-tee," repeats an itinerant hawker balancing a box of wood over a small cushion on his head. Like a procession of ants, we all proceed down Betances Street to the heart of the town. A woman is selling lottery tickets in front of the Polanco pharmacy. "A million dollar prize" she announces as she pursues people on the street. A man stops and she removes a pair of scissors from her pocket. At that moment the San Antonio bells announce eleven o'clock Mass. A flock of grey pigeons escape from the tower to take refuge in the trees of the plaza.

Then I remember you are with us...in my imagination, of course. I believe you are pleased to have joined us. There is so much about us that you do not know. I smile sweetly. I can now smile at you now because you no longer cause me pain. I understand you now. I remind you that you should understand Sara. Sara has her own life. And there is something else; something important I must say to you. I want you to forgive me. Yes, if I can help it. I don't want you to keep resenting me. It's too heavy a burden to bear on my account. I want you to enjoy the same sense of peace I'm beginning to feel. So I ask you to forgive my long absences, my lack of understanding, and my stubborn, blind bitterness, For all the suffering I caused you without meaning to, forgive me! The sound of my thoughts flows transparently, effortlessly, the three syllables, clear even though you are not here to listen to them. I am aware of the fantasy engendered by the dire need to open my heart to you. Even so, I want to believe that in some way, you and I go beyond and above the words that you could and tried to say to me. So, I ask again that you forgive me even if I never find out whether you have.

"Some houses look like shrouds." I whisper.

Esteban looks at me out of the corner of his eye. He has been whistling an old tune. "Around here?" he asks. He is not looking for an answer; he's in no mood for a discussion on urban planning.

"Yes. My house is in the circle as you turn the next corner," I say.

Nonetheless I sense that neither you nor he remembers it. You only visited twice. "It's hidden behind the big *flamboyan*," I add in the intimacy of our silence. My eyes follow the finger which in my imagination has acted as your guide to the house and they come upon the tree...

I can't stop admiring the abundance of bloom this year. It is a burst of vibrant red luminescence, both captivating and seductive. The old roots are covered by a carpet of fallen flowers. I have never seen it so lovely.

Esteban stops the jeep right under the *flamboyan*. I turn my eyes away from the small cluster of little red flowers, so crowded together that they look like tiny orchids. I look for the discolored tiles above the archway from force of habit, the ones which dominate the facade of the house. Sadly I see the deterioration and how abandoned and deserted it appears. The gate at the entrance has collapsed to one side, the hinges are warped by the salpeterous winds, the wooden railing of the balcony is rotted and the iron grillwork over the windows rusty. I hunt in my purse for the keys and walk toward Esteban pushing aside the will-of-the-wisp which has invaded the entrance to the house.

"Would you like some coffee?" he asks before he disappears under the cover of the hood.

I second the offer of the warm aromatic ritual. I turn the key automatically and listen to metal grinding over metal. I push the door open and discover familiar objects, there to receive me in the half shadow. Then I sense your presence. I hear your voice wrapped in the same tender tones you surely must have felt when first you suckled me at your breast:

"Mariana, I do forgive you!"